It's time for a
COWS IN ACTION!

Genius cow Professor McMoo and his
trusty sidekicks, Pat and Bo, are star
agents of the C.I.A. – short for
COWS IN ACTION!
They travel through time, fighting evil
bulls from the future and keeping
history on the right track . . .

Find out more at
www.cowsinaction.com

= don't know

C.I.A.

COWS IN ACTION

THE TER-MOO-NATORS

Steve Cole

Illustrated by Woody Fox

RED FOX

THE TER-MOO-NATORS
A RED FOX BOOK 978 1 862 30189 4

First published in Great Britain by Red Fox,
an imprint of Random House Children's Books

This edition published 2007

5 7 9 10 8 6

Set in Bembo Schoolbook by
Falcon Oast Graphic Art Ltd.

Red Fox Books are published by Random House Children's Books,
61–63 Uxbridge Road, London W5 5SA

www.**kids**at**randomhouse**.co.uk

Addresses for companies within
The Random House Group Limited can be found at:
www.randomhouse.co.uk/offices.htm

THE RANDOM HOUSE GROUP Limited Reg. No. 954009

The Random House Group Limited supports The Forest
Stewardship Council (FSC), the leading international forest
certification organisation. All our titles that are printed on
Greenpeace approved FSC certified paper carry the FSC logo.
Our paper procurement policy can be found at:
www.rbooks.co.uk/environment

A CIP catalogue record for this book is available from the British Library.

Printed in the UK by CPI Bookmarque, Croydon, CR0 4TD

For Tobey

With special thanks and
a golden Malteser to Mini Grey

Prof. McMoo's
TIMELINE OF NOTABLE
HISTORICAL EVENTS

4.6 billion years BC
PLANET EARTH FORMS
(good job too)

13.7 billion years BC
BIG BANG - UNIVERSE BEGINS
(and first tea atoms created)

23 million years BC
FIRST COWS APPEAR

(23 million is my lucky number!)

1700 BC
SHEN NUNG MAKES FIRST CUP OF TEA
(what a hero!)

7000 BC
FIRST CATTLE KEPT ON FARMS
(Not a great year for cows)

2550 BC
GREAT PYRAMID BUILT AT GIZA

(by an Egyptian geezer)

1901 AD
QUEEN VICTORIA DIES
(she was not a-moo-sed)

31 BC
ROMAN EMPIRE FOUNDED

(Roam-Moo empire founded by a cow but no one remembers that)

1509 AD
HENRY VIII COMES TO THE THRONE

(and probably squashes it)

1066 AD
BATTLE OF HASTINGS

(but what about the Cattle of Hastings?)

1620 AD
ENGLISH PILGRIMS SETTLE IN AMERICA

(bringing with them the first cows to moo in an American accent)

1939 AD
WORLD WAR TWO BEGINS

(or World War Moo as it is known to cows)

2007 AD
I INVENT A TIME MACHINE!!!

2500 AD
COW NATION OF LUCKYBURGER FOUNDED

(HOORAY!)

2550 AD
COWS IN ACTION RECRUIT PROFESSOR McMOO, PAT AND BO

(and now the fun REALLY starts...)

(about time!)

1903 AD
FIRST TEABAGS INVENTED

THE TER-MOO-NATORS

Chapter One

THE FARMYARD FURY

WHAP! The pig in the boxing gloves went flying through the air and landed with a splash in the duck pond. His opponent – a small goat – gave a puzzled bleat.

"Yay!" called Pat Vine, although he didn't really think that punching a pig was much to shout about. Especially when the goat had only done it by accident while struggling out of her boxing gloves.

Pat was a young, handsome bullock whose coat was light brown and covered with small white zigzags, and he was here to support his sister – a

3

dairy cow called Little Bo Vine. She needed a bit of cheering on at her self-defence classes. The other farm animals just sat there looking dozy.

"See, goat? You could be a brilliant boxer," said Little Bo approvingly as she fished out the pig from the pond. She had a rosy red and white coat and was very much a cow with attitude – lately she had taken to chewing bubble gum rather than cud, and dyeing her udder bright green. "But listen, pig – if you don't want to end up as battered bacon, you've got to put up more of a fight."

The pig stared at her blankly.

"In fact, you *all* have to put up more of a fight!" Bo yelled at the animals. "You're about as tough as a wet paper bag, the whole lot of you. And Bessie Barmer knows it. She is not just the farmer's wife, she is our public enemy number one!"

That's true, thought Pat with a shudder.

Farmer Barmer was nice enough, but
his wife, Bessie, hated all the animals on
the organic farm. She made their lives a
misery, and couldn't wait to turn them
all into hamburgers, hot dogs, cutlets
and chops.

The other animals didn't seem to
understand the deadly fate that awaited
them. But Bo and Pat belonged to a
rare breed of clever cattle called the

Emmsy-Squares, and they understood *lots* of things. Even so, they weren't the smartest cattle around. The brainiest bull in the whole world lived on the farm too.

The bull's name was Angus McMoo. *Professor* Angus McMoo, to be precise. And his shed was filled with history books and science papers on subjects Pat couldn't begin to understand.

"Where *is* the professor?" Bo asked her brother. "Don't tell me — he's got his head stuck in a book."

Pat peered down the hillside to the end of the field. "Nope. He's got his head stuck in a dustbin, actually."

"Again." Bo sighed.

Pat grinned as he watched Professor McMoo almost disappear inside one of the bins. He thought the professor was awesome.

McMoo was stocky and sharp and in the prime of his life. He was reddy-brown with large white box-shapes

patterning his hide – and had an incredible thirst for knowledge. A scientist lived in the house next door, and his garden just happened to back onto McMoo's paddock. This scientist chucked away all sorts of high-tech gear – computer chips, cables, levers and switches . . . And that was exactly what Professor McMoo needed for the super-secret, super-special project he was working on. Pat was dying to know what it was, but the professor just smiled and said, "You'll find out – in *time* . . ."

"He should stop fiddling about and learn how to look after himself more," Bo complained. "If Bessie Barmer catches him in the bins again she'll go crazy."

"Holy cow," cried Pat. "Here she comes now!"

There was no mistaking the enormous woman in the dirty duffel coat as she came bustling into the paddock. She was as fat as a hay bale, with a face like a sweaty boar sucking a dirty lemon. Her legs and arms were as thick as tree trunks, and each of her fearsome fists was the size of a piglet.

"Pro-fess-soooooooor!" mooed Little Bo at the top of her cow lungs. "Look out!"

McMoo ducked out of the dustbin and saw the danger he was in. He started hoofing it towards Pat, Bo and the others.

"Oi!" Bessie bellowed. "Come back here, you big burger on legs!"

At once, the farm animals fell into a panic, quacking, snorting and bleating like bonkers. "Don't let her scare you!" Bo urged them. "Stand up to her! Remember what I taught you all!"

But the sad truth was, the other animals were just too thick to learn anything. The ducks had ducked out of her Tae Kwon Do class, and the sheep were too busy guzzling grass to

9

master even basic judo. Pat watched the goat finally pull off her boxing gloves and scarper after the pig – just as Professor McMoo charged up, Bessie hard on his heels.

"Quick!" said the professor urgently, his voice muffled by a strange metal gadget in his mouth. "One of you hide this!"

He spat the gadget out onto the floor and Pat flopped down on top of it.

"What are you up to, beef-features?" squawked Bessie. "I've told you before, keep your snout out of those bins, or you'll be sorry!"

Before McMoo could react, Little Bo yawned noisily and went to the toilet right in front of Bessie.

"Ugh!" cried Bessie, backing away as her feet got splashed. "You should show me some respect! My ancestors mixed with royalty, you know!"

"Is that why you ended up as a royal pain in the bottom?" asked Pat – but to human ears, of course, it only sounded like a long, low *mooo-oo*. Bessie was always going on about her famous ancestors. But Professor McMoo was an expert on history and told Pat and Bo he had never heard of *any* important Barmers. Not ever.

Apparently, being an expert on history was vital to the success of his super-secret project . . .

Shaking her wet legs, her filthy mood getting filthier by the second, Bessie narrowed her tiny eyes at Pat and Bo. "What are *you* two looking at, you steaks-in-training?" She shook her fist at them. "Push off back to your own field. Now!"

"Moo-oo-ooo," mumbled Pat. He gave a sigh of relief as Bessie stomped off towards the farmhouse.

"Sorry to break up your self-defence

class, Bo," said Professor McMoo. "But well done for getting rid of her. There's no time to waste." He chuckled to himself mysteriously. "*Literally* no time to waste. Come on! Come with me. I've got something to show you, and there's no time like the present." He paused. "Or *is* there?"

Pat got up, a frown on his face. "What do you mean, Professor?"

"Yeah, what are you going on about?" Bo added as she peered down at the device Pat had squashed into the grass.

McMoo grabbed it in his mouth and set off for his shed, muttering to himself. "I *knew* that scientist would throw away a multigrade sprocket if I waited long enough . . ."

"Professor, what *are* you up to?" Pat shouted.

"Ha!" laughed McMoo. "Follow me and find out!"

Chapter Two

THE SECRET IN THE SHED

Bo and Pat followed the professor into his shed. It was empty except for a bed of hay and a pile of textbooks hidden behind a trough in the corner.

"I don't know why I bother with self-defence classes sometimes," Bo grumbled. "Everyone goes to pieces as soon as that bloomin' Bessie Barmer shows up."

"The other animals aren't clever like us," Pat reminded her. "Well, like me and the professor anyway!" he added cheekily.

"Watch it, small fry," said Bo, swiping him with her tail. "At least I know the

14

difference between a karate chop and a mutton chop – and that's more than you and him do!"

"You mean, 'you and *he* do'," the professor corrected her, fiddling about with his gadget from the dustbin.

"See?" said Pat. "Brains are better than brawn!"

"Are not!" Bo replied.

"Are too!" said Pat fiercely.

"Stop squabbling!" cried the professor. "Give me a round of applause instead."

"Why?" asked Bo.

"Because I've finally come up with a way for us all to escape that dratted Bessie Barmer for ever – that's why!" He crossed to a particular patch of straw on the floor and spat the sprocket into it. "Put the kettle on, Pat – this calls for a celebration cuppa!"

Pat smiled and did so. Professor McMoo loved his cups of tea. He had fixed a broken kettle he found in the scientist's dustbin, and now, each week, Bo sneaked into the farmhouse kitchen to "borrow" tea bags.

Bo raised her eyebrows as McMoo got on with warming the teapot. "So you've finished this super-secret project then, Professor? Where is it?"

McMoo chuckled. "You're standing in it!"

Standing in things was often unavoidable for cows and those around them, but Little Bo could see nothing on her hooves. "What?"

"This whole *place* is my super-secret project!" cried McMoo. He perched a pair of glasses on his nose, ran to the other end of the shed and kicked away an old sack to reveal a big bronze lever.

Bo frowned. "So. Big whoop. You built a lever."

"That's so cool," said Pat loyally.

"It's not just *any* lever," said McMoo with pride. "It's the CHURN lever. Watch!"

He gave it a hard yank — and a loud, rattling, clanking sound started up.

Pat threw tea bags in the air as part of the wooden wall behind him spun round to reveal switches and buttons and flashing lights on the other side. A large computer screen swung down from the rafters. Bo was bumped on the bottom by a horseshoe-shaped bank of controls rising out from the hay-covered ground, filling the middle of the shed.

McMoo laughed with glee — and Pat and Bo stared in amazement — as hidden panels, covered in cables and levers and read-outs swung round into view on every wall. In ten seconds flat, the ordinary, empty cow shed had changed into an incredible futuristic control centre, throbbing and glowing with a strange power.

"Wow!" Pat exclaimed. "What just happened?"

"The CHURN lever works!" McMoo beamed at his two young friends. "Blimey, I'm brilliant. CHURN, you see – stands for Controls Hidden Under Revolving . . . um, Nanels."

"Nanels?" echoed Bo. "What are nanels, then?"

McMoo sighed as he picked up the tea bags. "Well, really it should be 'Panels'. But that would make it a CHURP lever, and that sounds silly."

"Who cares what it's called?" cried Pat. "It's incredible!" He trotted about in excitement, staring at the different "nanels". "But what do these controls actually do, Professor?"

"You are no longer standing in an ordinary cow shed," said Professor McMoo. "I have turned it into . . . a *time machine!*"

"A time machine?" Pat whispered, wide-eyed.

Bo snorted. "You've been eating funny grass again."

"It's true, I tell you," said McMoo. "With the Time Shed we can escape this boring old farm and Bessie Bloomin' Barmer, and go anywhere on Earth. We can pop off to the past or fly into the future." His brown eyes sparkled as he looked at his two friends. "So! Ready for the test-drive?"

"Yes! Yes!" said Pat, jumping up and down.

"Is it going to blow up?" said Bo cautiously.

"Only if I press that big blue button there," said McMoo with a grin. "Don't worry, we're perfectly safe. This is the finest technology money can buy."

"But you didn't buy it!" she argued. "You found it in a bin!"

"True," McMoo agreed, filling the

teapot with hot water. "But it was a very fine and expensive bin."

"Come on, Bo," said Pat. "It'll be an adventure!"

"I suppose I better had come along," said Bo, looking between McMoo and her brother. "You'll need me to keep an eye on you."

"As if!" Pat snorted.

"Enough chat!" McMoo strode into the horseshoe of controls, set down the teapot and hit some switches with his snout. "I'll just set the controls to take us back a hundred years, to see what the farm was like back then. Rolling fields, no Bessie Barmer, nice cup of tea. Perfect combination!" He curled his tail around a big red lever. "Here we go, then . . ."

But before he could pull it down, a strange cloud of black smoke appeared from nowhere behind him.

"Um, is that *meant* to happen,

Professor?" asked Pat.

McMoo whirled round. A huge, dark, menacing shape could be seen inside the smoke.

"Looks like a bull," said Bo uneasily. "A very big one."

The smoke faded and the figure stepped forward from the large silver plate it stood on. It was no ordinary bull. It had steel-grey horns, and eyes glowing green. Robotic parts had been added to its legs and body. Its tail was a metal spike.

And it was pointing a large ray gun straight at Professor McMoo!

Chapter Three

ATTACK FROM THE FUTURE!

"Aaagh!" yelled Pat. "Where did you spring from?"

"I am a ter-moo-nator," said the mysterious bull in a low, grating voice. "I have come from hundreds of years in the future. I have been sent to destroy Professor Angus McMoo."

Bo frowned. "You what?"

"No!" Pat shouted, his legs trembling. "You can't hurt the professor!"

The ter-moo-nator smiled nastily. "Can too!"

But McMoo himself seemed delighted. "This robo-bull has heard of me!" he cried. "In the future, I must be famous.

Imagine that!"

"You will be destroyed," the ter-moo-nator repeated.

"Ah. Yes. Hmm." McMoo's smile dropped. "I'm less happy about that bit."

"Why do you want to destroy him, anyway?" asked Pat.

The ter-moo-nator stalked towards Professor McMoo. "Because he is going to become the greatest enemy of the F.B.I."

"The F.B.I.?" McMoo scratched his head. "Those American law-enforcers?"

"No, not *that* F.B.I.," said the menacing creature. "*This* F.B.I. stands for the *Fed-up Bull Institute*!"

"I'm getting pretty fed-up myself," said McMoo, folding his arms. "You barge in here, waving a big gun about, going on about destroying me—"

"YOU *SHALL* BE DESTROYED!" roared the ter-moo-nator, and both Bo and Pat took a step backwards in alarm. "I shall turn you into beef-flavoured mush!"

"Mush, you say?" Professor McMoo frowned. "Oh dear, dear, *dear* Mr Ter-moo-nator, please hold your horses. Or your cows, or chickens, or whatever it is ter-moo-nators hold. You've travelled several hundred years to squish me, haven't you? You must be worn out. How about a nice cup of tea before you blast me into steak atoms, eh?"

Pat and Bo stared at the professor, flabbergasted.

"Tea?" the ter-moo-nator repeated suspiciously.

"I've just brewed a fresh pot," said McMoo with an innocent smile. "Try some!"

And suddenly he hurled the teapot at the ter-moo-nator, conking him right on the head.

"Bull's-eye!" cried Pat.

"Well, bull's-lower-forehead to be precise," the professor corrected him.

The robotic bull staggered back with an angry snort, raising its gun.

But Bo sprang into action with her own special brand of self-defence. "D'you want some milk to go with that tea?" She reared up and blasted the monster with milk from her day-glo udder. The ter-moo-nator glubbed and blubbed and dropped its gun as the milk splashed into its mouth and eyes.

Pat gazed in astonishment at his brave sister. Maybe brawn was OK as well as brains – and maybe if he applied one to the other . . .

Taking a deep breath, Pat charged up

to the stricken bull. "And now – sugar!"

"Don't call me sugar," growled the ter-moo-nator.

"One *lump* or two?" said Pat, whacking the ter-moo-nator twice on the head with his front hooves. Sparks crackled around the monster's silver horns.

"Nice one, Pat," yelled Bo, running forward. "But *three* lumps will make him even sweeter!"

"Aim for the central flange unit housed in his rump!" McMoo instructed.

Bo paused, mid-charge. "You what?"

"Kick the controls in his bum!" Pat translated.

Bo did as she was told, landing a hefty kick to the round metal machine in the robotic bull's butt. The controls sparked and smoked and the ter-moo-nator went cross-eyed. "Mission abort!" it warbled, covered in milk and tea, jerking back to its silver plate. "Malfunction! Recall! Mission abort!"

"Ha!" shouted Bo. "The beef's come to grief!"

And in a puff of black smoke, the bull from the future vanished.

Pat and Bo joined McMoo, staring at the empty space where the half-metal monster had been standing.

"Good punching, Pat," Bo cheered.

"And that was an excellent roundhouse kick, Bo," the professor noted. "Superb."

She blushed. "I never thought you paid attention in my kickboxing class, Professor. You always seemed to be reading."

"My dear Bo, I'm a genius, remember?" McMoo nudged her in the ribs. "I can do seven things at once. Doing two is a doddle!"

"Where do you think that thing came from, Professor?" said Pat shakily.

"I don't know," said McMoo. "But I must admit, I haven't been so scared since Bessie Barmer's extra-big pants blew off the washing line and hit me in the face!"

Pat shuddered at the thought. But the ter-moo-nator was an even scarier thought than Bessie's bloomers. "Do you think that robo-bull thing is . . . dead?"

McMoo shook his head. "You heard it say 'recall'. I think it's been transported away. Taken back to wherever it came from."

"Correct!" came a booming moo from behind them. "Back to the future!"

Professor McMoo spun round. Two cows were standing in the open doorway to the Time Shed, panting for breath like they had been running. They were dressed in black suits, cool dark shades and pointy hats like a wizard's, only smaller. The only way you could tell them apart was that one was bigger than the other.

"More ter-moo-nators?" cried Bo, raising her hooves.

"Uh-oh." Pat gulped. "If only we had another teapot."

"If only we had Bessie Barmer's extra-big pants!" Bo exclaimed.

"There is no need for tea *or* pants," said the biggest cow quickly. "We are not ter-moo-nators."

Bo stared at them suspiciously. "But you *are* from the future, aren't you?"

"Yes," admitted the cow.

Pat was impressed. "How did you know, Bo?"

"Easy," she told him. "No cow in this century would be seen dead wearing a hat like that!"

"Er, can we come in?" asked the larger cow.

"No!" Professor McMoo stood protectively in front of Pat and Bo. "What are you cows of the future doing here in our time? Eh? What's going on?"

"We came here to save you, Angus McMoo," said the smaller of the two cows in an even deeper voice. "You and your Time Shed."

McMoo frowned. "Have you been spying on me?"

"We have always known that you built a time machine," said the first cow, "because for us, it has already happened, long ago."

The second cow nodded. "We are cows from the year 2550 – and you must travel there with us. At once!"

Pat and Bo stared in utter amazement.

"Why?" asked McMoo pointedly.

"Are you sure we can't come in?" said

the smaller cow. "In one-point-three minutes it will start raining, and we haven't got our coats."

"You just stay where you are!" McMoo stomped up to the curious cows in the doorway. "I don't want to seem bullish about this – although I am a bull, obviously – but this is my Time Shed!" He frowned at them. "Perhaps in your time, everyone has their own magic time-travelling silver platter. But right now, in *this* time, a time machine is a bit special, OK? And I'm using it to escape from this farm – not running a taxi service for cows on their way to a fancy-dress party!"

"We wear the uniform of the Prime Moo-vers," said the biggest cow grandly. "I am Shetland."

"And I am Holstein," said his friend.

"What's a Prime Moo-ver?" asked Pat.

"We rule kindly over all cattle," said Holstein.

"Well you don't rule us!" Bo replied. It was bad enough being bossed around by Bessie Barmer, without these weird cows joining in.

"We don't want to rule you," said Holstein patiently. "We came to save you. When we learned that the F.B.I. had sent a ter-moo-nator to get Professor McMoo, we hoofed it over here in a flash."

Shetland nodded. "Those Fed-up Bulls know that you are all destined to be star agents of the C.I.A."

"C.I.A.?" McMoo blinked. "You mean the Central Intelligence Agency in America?"

"No," said Shetland. "I mean *Cows in Action* – a crack team of time-travelling cow commandos, dedicated to saving the world!"

Chapter Four

FUTURE COW PARADISE

"Pull the udder one!" Little Bo glared at the strange future cows. "Why should we believe anything you say?"

But just then it started to rain – exactly as Holstein had predicted. The two suited cows sighed in the open doorway as their sunglasses started to steam up.

"Well, OK then, we can believe *some* of the things you say," said Pat. "But if you came from the future to save us from that nasty bull-thing, how come you turned up too late to do anything?"

Holstein looked forlorn. "Our time machine broke down. We couldn't get the doors open, so we got here late."

"It was really embarrassing," Shetland admitted.

McMoo brightened. "I'm clever with machines. In fact, I'm clever full stop! I'll soon fix it for you."

"Impossible." Holstein shook rainwater from his head. "When it broke down, we set it to self-destruct. Technology from the twenty-sixth century must never fall into the hands of humans in the twenty-first."

"Why not?" Pat wondered.

"Because they are not ready for it," said Shetland. "Suppose I crash-landed a fighter jet in medieval times, and the humans there learned its secrets. Imagine what such violent, primitive people would do with rocket engines, air-to-ground missiles, computers . . ."

McMoo nodded gravely. "They would have amazing technology, but not the wisdom to use it," he said. "They could destroy their world a hundred times over."

"Exactly," said Holstein. He licked a dangling raindrop from his nose. "Careless time travel can change the course of history and destroy the future!"

"And we have enough on our hooves trying to stop the F.B.I. from doing exactly that," said Shetland. "You see, Professor, thanks to you, future cows know the secrets of time travel. But we

Prime Moo-vers place heavy restrictions on its use. We observe historical events, but rarely interfere."

"Quite right too," said McMoo approvingly.

"The F.B.I. are different," said Holstein. "They do nothing *but* interfere! When we wouldn't let them use our Time Sheds, they built their own miniature time machines instead."

"We saw one," Pat revealed. "Looked like a big silver disc."

Bo nodded. "First time I ever saw beef serve itself up on a plate!"

"A ter-moo-nator is *cyber*-beef," said Shetland gravely. "The F.B.I. took their meanest, nastiest members and made them stronger and smarter with robotic parts."

"Now they are the perfect time-travelling agents," added Holstein. "Ruthless, fearless and programmed to win at all costs." He shook a soggy suit-sleeve and sighed. "Now *please* can we come in out of the rain?"

"Oi," came the familiar screech of Bessie Barmer from outside. "Where did you two cows come from?"

"All right," McMoo agreed. "And you'd better shut the door too – fast!"

"Cows in silly costumes indeed," Bessie snarled. "Well, Ted the Butcher will take

them whatever they're wearing . . ."

"B-b-butcher?" Holstein turned as white as a ghost and slammed the door. "We don't have butchers in our own time!"

Pat's ears pricked up. "You don't?"

Shetland shook his head. "Cows and humans live together as equals. We enjoy long lives and the freedom to roam wherever we like."

"Wow!" Bo beamed. "Sounds good!"

"Please, Professor," said Holstein. "Will you let us show you our future world – and your destiny?"

All eyes were on McMoo.

"Do they still have tea in the twenty-sixth century?" he asked.

"We shall send a moo-ssenger to fetch the finest tea bags in China," cried Shetland. "Only *please* come!"

A harsh, scraping sound came from just outside – the sound of big knives being sharpened. "Oh, little stray cooooooooo-ws," called Bessie Barmer in a sing-song voice. "Come out to play! Auntie Bessie's got something for yoooooooooou . . ."

"Quick, Professor!" said Pat. "Before she comes inside!"

"It seems I have no choice," said McMoo. He crossed to the control centre and set the date. "Year: 2550. Location . . . ?"

"Sunflower Drive, Luckyburger," Holstein told him.

"Luckyburger?" Bo spluttered.

"In your time it is the country known as Luxembourg," said Shetland. "But in the twenty-sixth century it is called Luckyburger, and only cows live there."

"I don't believe it," said Pat in a daze.

"Then let's see it for ourselves." McMoo's tail curled around the red take-off lever, and he grinned at his companions. "Stand by for that test-drive. We're going over five hundred years into our own future!"

He yanked hard on the lever. There was a hum of power. And then a whine. And then a deep, throaty roar. The shed began to vibrate.

"What are you up to in there?" shouted Bessie Barmer, but her voice was fading away, replaced by a swooshing, swishing, hissing sound. It was the sound of time itself surging and splashing like a vast, mysterious ocean against the sturdy walls of the Time Shed as the little building sped into the future.

Blinding bright light peeped in through cracks in the wood. The control centre juddered and shuddered, harder and faster.

Little Bo's udder started wobbling like lime-green jelly. "I've heard of a milkshake, but this is ridiculous!" she groaned.

"Nearly there," gasped Professor McMoo, his eyes on the time-o-meter.

The years were whizzing by – 2456,
2498, 2521, 2539 . . .

Suddenly there was a crash like a
thousand milk bottles dropping off a
cliff. The Time Shed rocked and rattled

and squealed as it dumped itself back into reality.

Pat breathed a long sigh of relief. "We made it!"

"Ha-haaaaa!" McMoo jumped in the air with happiness. "The Time Shed works – we've actually *moo-oo-oo*ved through time and space!"

Bo gave him a look. "So you say."

"If the professor says we've moved, then we've moved!" Pat said loyally.

"There's one way to check." Holstein crossed to the doors and sniffed suspiciously. Then he threw them open. "Ahh, yes. Smell that air, so rich with cowpats!"

"We are home," Shetland cried. "Welcome to Luckyburger, one and all!"

McMoo crossed quickly to the doors and reached them just ahead of Bo and Pat. All three of them followed the Prime Moo-vers outside – and stared round in wonder.

They found themselves in the middle
of a road made of fragrant wild grass.
Huge sunflowers grew alongside. Cows
and oxen, bulls and buffalos, cattle of all
different breeds and sizes wandered
happily through the
lush green
meadows that
stretched on
for miles
around.
Shetland
walked
up to a
cow in
a blue
cap and

47

murmured in its ear. The cow jumped onto a sort of silver scooter, which suddenly sped off into the sky.

"That's what I call getting on your bike!" said McMoo approvingly. "Anti-gravity motors under the saddle, eh? I wish I'd thought of that!"

"You will," Holstein informed him. "In about five years from now."

"The Time Shed is only the first of your great inventions," Shetland added. "Many of them are still used today."

McMoo beamed. "Tell me, do I ever manage to invent an electric sundial?" he asked hopefully.

Shetland and Holstein swapped puzzled looks. "Er, no."

"Oh." Professor McMoo looked a bit forlorn, but quickly brightened. "Oh well, maybe someone will think of it one day!"

Pat shook his aching head. It was hard enough coming to terms with being in a new time and place, without the added distraction of wondering how an electric sundial would work. But just then a massive, juicy-looking clump of grass caught his eye. He licked his lips, all cares suddenly forgotten.

"Help yourself, young Pat," boomed Holstein. "Everything is free here."

"This place is all right, I suppose," said Bo, noisily chewing her gum. "But it would be better with some loud music."

Holstein smiled politely. "Perhaps you will like our home better, the Palace of Great Moos."

"Does it have a cool stereo?" she asked excitedly. "Amusement arcade? Indoor swimming pool? A milkmaid with warm hands to massage your udder?"

"Not as such," Shetland admitted. "But it's ever so nice."

"Nice?" Bo looked horrified. "Ugh!"

Holstein cleared his throat politely. "This road takes us straight there. Shall we go?"

McMoo took in the clear blue sky, the tweeting birds, the fresh air and the sheer amount of tasty grub all around him, and gave a deep, contented sigh. "It's a cow paradise, all right," he declared as they all set off along the grassy track. "So tell me. How did all this start?"

"It started with *you*, McMoo. You were the first cow genius to ever be born." Holstein smiled. "The Emmsy-Squares

were the *first* breed of clever cattle, but others soon followed . . . The Piedish Shorthorns, the Cloven Wagglehooves . . . Slowly but surely, cows, oxen, bulls and heifers all revealed their intelligence. They made little improvements around their farms. They started to help with the accounts."

Shetland took up the story. "But it was only when a bison stood for election as governor of Alabama in 2213 that people really started to look at cattle in a different light."

"Did he win?" asked McMoo.

"No, he was disqualified for butting his opponent's wife at a rally," said Holstein sadly. "But a Welsh Black was elected to the British House of Commons soon after. Humans finally came to realize there was more to cows than roast beef and milk."

"But not all cows were grateful to the humans for giving us this land," said

Shetland. "Some wanted revenge for all those centuries of being treated like . . . er, cattle. So they formed the *Fed-up Bull Institute* – the F.B.I. Their mission is to wipe out human history and make the Age of the Clever Cow begin far sooner."

Bo shrugged. "So? Sounds like a pretty good plan to me."

Her words had a strange effect. The Prime Moo-vers started mooing like foghorns, trotting around in circles and getting themselves in a real state.

"Meddling with the past can only lead to disaster!" cried Shetland.

"But it could work out really cool for cows everywhere!" Bo protested.

"No," said Holstein firmly. "Every time the past is changed, so is the future. Imagine if you took the Time Shed to see how this farm looked a hundred years ago – but landed on top of the farmer, and squashed him flat. His wife might sell the farm. It could end up as a shopping centre or a car park."

"I see what you mean," said Pat, frowning. "If it wasn't a farm, we wouldn't ever have been there. And that means the professor would never have found the bits and pieces in next-door's bins that he needed to build the Time Shed . . ."

Holstein nodded. "And you would all have been zapped out of existence in a second."

"Hmm. Good job I would never dream of taking the Time Shed on such a foolhardy trip, eh?" McMoo said quickly, ignoring the looks Bo was giving him. "So, let me see if I've got this straight. Basically, if the horrid history of cows is changed in any way, then this fabulous future awaiting us all may never happen."

"That's right," said Shetland, a little calmer now. "You three are the first of the Clever Cows. Will you agree to help us safeguard the future? Will you join the fight against the F.B.I.? Will you join the C.I.A. and become Cows in Action?"

"From Bull Genius to Clever Cow." Professor McMoo scratched his head. "Crikey. What have I got us all into?"

"An adventure and a half by the sound of it!" Little Bo grinned. "Count me in."

"And me," agreed Pat, chewing heroically on some clover.

"And me too, I suppose." McMoo sighed. "On one condition."

"What is that?" asked Shetland, smiling.

"That I get some tea, pronto!" cried McMoo. He winked at Pat and Bo. "How can I fight deadly robot bulls with a mouth as dry as dung in the desert?"

Then they all ducked as the cow in

the blue cap went whizzing overhead on her scooter, a big sack marked TEA BAGS swung over one shoulder.

Pat stared in wonder. "Has that cow been to China and back *already*?"

"What's more, she probably stopped for a weed sandwich along the way." Shetland grinned. "She's going to the palace."

"And so are we!" McMoo declared, whisking Pat and Bo away with him along the grassy track at a fast gallop.

Shetland and Holstein stared after the bossy, brainy bull and his friends. Smiles spread slowly over their faces. It looked as if the C.I.A. had just gained three very unusual members!

Chapter Five

CATTLE SET FOR BATTLE

Around the next bend in the grassy road, the Palace of Great Moos came into sight. "Huh!" said Bo, but McMoo and Pat gazed upon it in wonder.

The palace was a large dome made of milk-white marble, set in a sprawling courtyard. Towers and turrets rose from it like enormous horns, pointing up into the sky. All around, magnificent fountains gushed and burbled. The grounds were lined with huge hedges, cut into the shape of giant milk churns and cows in heroic poses.

"That is where we Prime Moo-vers live and work," said Holstein. "And

where C.I.A. has its headquarters."

"Have you thought about painting it bright yellow?" Bo asked. "Or spray-painting some cool graffiti on the walls?"

"No," said Shetland flatly.

The band of cows went through grass-green doors in the great marble dome and clomped into a large, cool entrance hall. Ahead of them was a glittering gold door, and huge water troughs were lined up against the walls on either side. To McMoo's delight, one of the troughs was full of fresh, steaming hot tea. "At last!" he boomed. Then he stuck his head in it and happily slurped it all down.

Bo stood beside Shetland at the water trough. "So who is your leader?" she asked, sticking her gum behind her ear.

"The wisest cow on Earth," said Shetland.

"*My name is Madame Milkbelly the Third!*"

The prim voice echoed around the hall as the gold door slid open – to reveal a very big and very old cow. Her black and white coat was saggy and wrinkled, and her udder was the size of a small Labrador. She wore dark glasses and – rather surprisingly – a huge silver nose ring.

The Prime Moo-vers all bowed down before her. McMoo and Pat quickly did

the same. But Bo stayed standing and grinned at her.

"All right, Madame Milky!" she said. "That's a wicked nose ring! Where did you get it?" The Prime Moo-vers gasped at her cheekiness. But Madame Milkbelly only smiled.

"I'm glad you like it," she said. "It is very big, because *I* am very big. The one *you* will have to wear is much smaller."

Pat looked at McMoo. "But, Professor, I thought only bulls needed nose rings?"

"You will *all* wear a special nose ring from now on," said a hefty black bull with large curly horns, striding out on his back legs from behind Madame Milkbelly. He wore a dark suit and shades like the Prime Moo-vers, but with a bright blue sash around his waist. He scattered three spangly silver nose rings onto the marble floor.

"Who are you?" wondered Pat.

"The name's Yak," growled the tough-looking bull. "I work for Madame M. and the Moo-vers — and now you will be working for me. I'm Director of the C.I.A."

"Pleased to meet you," said McMoo, picking up one of the rings. "What do you call these then?"

"Ringblenders," said Yak. "Standard C.I.A. equipment. They allow you to blend in with human beings when you travel back through time, so you don't stand out – so long as you are wearing the right clothes."

"Incredi-bull," McMoo murmured, studying his ringblender closely.

"They can also translate any language," added Madame Milkbelly. "So human beings in all times and places will understand you when you talk."

"And we will be able to understand them too!" said Pat, boggling.

"Never mind all this posh clever stuff," said Bo, clipping the silver ring to her nose as she turned to Yak. "What *I* want to know is – where did you get that sash from?"

"It's a special sash that shows you are a C.I.A. agent," he said. "You must wear one too."

Bo considered. "Could I maybe dye it pink and cut some holes in it?"

Shetland, Holstein and Madame Milkbelly burst into scandalized moos.

"No," said Yak. He offered neatly folded sashes to Bo, Pat and Professor McMoo. "Well, put them on, troops," he added. "It's time for your first mission."

"But we haven't had any training!" Pat protested.

Shetland looked shifty. "Unfortunately, no other C.I.A. agents are available."

"That's why *we* had to come and fetch you from your own time," Holstein explained. "Normally we would stay here ruling. But Yak is very short-staffed."

"All gone off on holiday, have they?" asked McMoo.

Yak shook his head. "They are all either squished, squashed or in hospital! Ter-moo-nators have super robotic strength and they fight well."

"Rubbish!" Bo snorted. "The one we met was pants! He couldn't arm wrestle a limp thistle."

"You got lucky," Yak told her grimly.

"Even so, Yak," put in Madame Milkbelly, "you must admit that our new special agents have one big advantage over the others." She grinned at Bo. "They have been taught self-defence by the most wild and wilful cow I've ever met!"

"Cheers, Madam M.!" Bo beamed. "Believe me, when you share a farm with Bessie Barmer, a ter-moo-nator is cuddly in comparison!"

"Now, what is this mission, Yak?" asked McMoo.

Yak turned to him. "Our spies have learned that the F.B.I. is holding a secret meeting in the city. They are getting ready to send another ter-moo-nator into the past – together with an unknown special agent."

"They must have found another weak point in time," guessed Madame Milkbelly. "A moment in history where things could easily change, allowing the F.B.I. to take control . . ." She looked at Professor McMoo, Pat and Bo in turn. "Those burly beefheads must not succeed. So get *moo*-ving, cows — it's time for action!"

Chapter Six

BULLS IN A CHINA SHOP!

Pat's heart beat faster as he followed Professor McMoo to the China Shop, a small store on a backstreet of the city – and the F.B.I.'s meeting place.

"This is a brilliant laugh, isn't it?" said Bo, trotting along happily beside him.

Pat frowned at her. "You should be wearing your C.I.A. sash."

"Get real! Blue is *so* not my colour." Instead, Bo had gone shopping for a shocking-pink crocodile-skin jacket and bright red boots. And she had dyed her udder purple.

"I've never had an agent dress that way before," grumbled Yak, who was marching along behind them.

"Talk to the hoof, mister," said Bo, blowing a bubble-gum bubble that popped in his face. "I'm doing you a favour by joining your silly C.I.A., curly-horns. So make like a fly and get off my back!"

Yak stared at her, speechless.

"Look on the bright side, Yak," said Professor McMoo. "The F.B.I. agents will be so busy staring at her, they'll be easier to catch!"

"Let's hope so," said Yak, recovering himself. He called them to a halt at the bottom of the street. "Now, here's the plan. You, Bo and Pat will go in the front way and drive out the F.B.I. agents. I will stay out here and arrest them when they run out."

"But there might be *lots* of F.B.I. agents," said Pat.

"There's a lot of me too, boy!" Yak puffed out his enormous chest. "And since I haven't got any more troops, I'll just have to cope. Good luck, guys."

The three C.I.A. agents trotted towards the shop. Professor McMoo tried the front door – but it was locked.

"How can we open it, Professor?" asked Bo.

"I think I'd better use my head," said McMoo. And then, lowering his horns, he went charging through the door – smashing it to matchwood!

A large white bull was standing guard, and true to his organization he looked pretty fed-up. With a moo of angry surprise, he started to charge at McMoo. But thinking fast, Pat tripped him up and Little Bo socked him over the horns with a double-hoofed blow. The white bull staggered backwards into a big pile of crockery, smashing it to pieces. Then he turned and ran through a large black door.

"Come on," commanded McMoo. "After him!"

The professor led the charge through the doorway into a large storeroom.

"Wait!" called Bo. "I can hear something."

Pat paused. A loud whirring, buzzing noise was coming from somewhere

overhead. "Either they have very, very large flies in this century . . ."

"Or there's a helicopter coming into land!" McMoo yelled, setting off at a gallop. He burst into a back room full of computers and flip charts and projector screens – and through a wide-open skylight above them, the C.I.A. agents could see a sleek helicopter rising up into the sky. Six huge bulls were dangling from a rope-ladder hanging beneath it. The big white one waved and jeered at them.

"Curdled cud!" Pat exclaimed. "We were just too late!"

'It seems the F.B.I. agents were ready for a quick getaway," agreed McMoo.

"And look, Professor!" Pat pointed to a faint cloud of black smoke in the corner of the room. "That's like the smoke we saw in the Time Shed."

McMoo nodded gravely. "I think the F.B.I. have already sent their troublemaking ter-moo-nator and his special agent friend into the past."

"Pants!" Bo stamped her hoof. "We've messed up our first mission."

"It's my fault really." They all whirled round – but it was only Yak. He looked very gloomy. "I didn't think that group of bulls would have their own helicopter."

McMoo sighed. "Well, at least we forced them to clear out in a hurry. Perhaps they left a clue behind. Let's see . . ."

"Actually, Pat's very good at finding things," said Bo.

"Yes, I'm sure he is, but we must start a careful search." Professor McMoo concentrated. "Now, based on the size of the room, I think we should split into teams of two and each tackle an area of 1.3475 metres—"

"What's this, Professor?" said Pat, picking up a small electronic gadget from the floor by his hoof.

McMoo blinked. "Good grief – it looks like a place-date data chip!"

71

"The Fed-up Bulls must have dropped it during their getaway," Yak realized.

"But what does it do?" asked Pat.

"It's like a date-and-location setter for a time machine," the professor explained. "Their silly silver platters are too small to have built-in controls, so it's all done by remote. But if I can use this to set the controls of my time machine, we can follow that ter-moo-nator to wherever he's going!"

Bo laughed. "I *told* you Pat was good at finding things!"

"Trouble, mostly," said Pat with a grin.

"Quick," said McMoo. He rushed them both away, with Yak hot on his hooves. "To the Time Shed – fast!"

It didn't take the brilliant, brainy bull professor long to work out that the data chip was set for a landing in Hampton Court – an old palace near London – on 27 December 1539.

"That's where King Henry the Eighth often stayed!" McMoo realized, back inside the Time Shed.

"Who?" said Bo blankly.

McMoo sighed. "Computer – give us the Henry the Eighth file."

Writing appeared on the big screen hanging down from the shed's rafters.

++Henry VIII. Born 1491, died 1547. ++King of England. ++Second ruling monarch of the Tudor family. ++Most powerful and dangerous king who ever lived. ++Ruled for 38 years. ++Started off thin, ended up VERY FAT. ++Father of Edward VI, Bloody Mary and Queen Elizabeth I.
++Famous for marrying six wives – Catherine of Aragon, Anne Boleyn, Jane Seymour, Anne of Cleves, Catherine Howard and Catherine Parr.

"He sounds nice," said Pat, without much enthusiasm.

"He sounds busy!" Bo decided.

"I'll sort out some special Tudor costumes for you," said Yak. "Then your ringblenders will allow you to walk among humans without them knowing you are cows."

"Will the ter-moo-nator have one too?" asked Bo.

"Yes," said Yak. "But don't forget, ringblenders only work on human eyes. You will be able to see through the ter-moo-nator's disguise — but he will be able to see through yours too."

"Can't you come with us, Yak?" asked Pat nervously. "You're used to tangling with ter-moo-nators."

"I wish I could," he said. "But Madame Milkbelly needs me here in case of an F.B.I. attack in our own time."

"I reckon she just likes looking at you in that flashy sash," said Bo, giving him a wink. "She fancies you, Yak!"

Yak blushed and stomped off quickly to check on the Tudor outfits — which had just arrived by cow-scooter. Soon the

C.I.A.'s best – and at the moment, *only* – agents were trying on the strange clothes.

"Ouch!" said Pat, trying to fasten a frilly ruff around his neck. "This is itchy!"

"And this gown will cover up my udder," Bo complained, wriggling into her dress. "I only just dyed it!"

"I think I look rather dashing!" said Professor McMoo, admiring his feathered hat and stripy stockings. "Now come on. There's no *time* to lose – well, apart from the thousand-odd years between now and 1539." He chuckled. "Tudor England, imagine that! I can't wait. I really can't wait!"

Yak frowned. "This is not a tourist trip, Professor. It's a vital mission."

"Yeah, yeah." Bo blew another big pink bubble. "You're always yakking, Yak!"

"When you're in the past, it's vital you don't change a thing," he went on,

ignoring her. "Just stop whatever it is the ter-moo-nator is up to and get out of there fast."

"Not even a *bit* of sightseeing?" McMoo looked disappointed.

Yak shook his head. "Not unless you want Madame Milkbelly coming down on you harder than a concrete cowpat."

McMoo winced. "That would hurt. OK. We'll be careful."

"Excuse me, Yak," said Pat. "What happens if a human from Tudor times wanders in and finds all this amazing technology? Couldn't that change history too?"

"I've already thought of that," said the professor, looking quite pleased with himself. "I've made the controls security coded. If anyone so much as tries to flick a switch without permission, the systems will self-destruct."

"Nice work," said Yak approvingly, strutting over to the shed doors. "Never forget, guys – the whole of history and the future safety of all cowkind is in your hooves."

The doors closed behind him.

Pat sighed. "No pressure then!"

"Don't worry, bruv," said Bo, more softly. "We'll deal with that beef-brained bull-bot, no sweat."

"I hope so," said McMoo, yanking down on the big red lever. Power surged through the shed as it began its familiar shaking. "Because whatever that ter-moo-nator is up to, we're the only ones who can stop it!"

Chapter Seven

TUDOR CUD

The Time Shed blazed back into existence in a cold, quiet courtyard. It was the middle of winter and very dark.

"We've arrived," said Professor McMoo, dancing around the shed like his hooves were stuffed with firecrackers. "At last, we've pitched up in the past! I've been dreaming of this for years. Tudor kings! Brave explorers! Unbelievably smelly toilets! All of that, out there waiting!"

"The toilets can *stay* waiting," said Bo, turning up her nose. "Ugh!"

"If a ter-moo-nator comes after me I might need one in a hurry," Pat confessed.

"Go now before we leave," Bo advised.

"Just don't splash the tea bags," called McMoo.

"We'd better stick those ringblender thingies on," said Bo, clipping hers in place. She had "decorated" it with pink and green nail varnish but luckily it still worked.

Pat finished his business and clipped his own ringblender into place. "Let's see what we look like," he said, crossing to a special mirror that Yak had given them. It showed the way they would appear to human eyes.

"Wow," said Bo, eyeing her reflection. She looked just like a Tudor lady! "Look at me – beef in a bodice! I make a pretty funky person, if I do say so myself."

Pat grinned at his handsome human reflection. "From bullock to baron, in the blink of an eye. And, Professor, look at you!"

McMoo smiled. "From a no-bull bull to a noble*man*!" The professor's reflection was lordly as you like. The mirror showed a large, powerful-looking man with curly hair and a huge moustache.

"Well, that's quite enough gawping in the mirror." He pulled on the CHURN-lever and all the fantastic technology vanished back into the walls and floor – if anyone forced their way inside they would see just a wooden building. "Let's see what's outside. Filth! Plague! No potatoes! Oooh, I do love history!"

"I'll love it better when that *ter-moo-nator* is history," said Bo.

"Er, Professor?" asked Pat nervously. "If this is the king's palace, won't people wonder what we're doing here and, um, try to lock us up and kill us and things?"

"Not if they don't see us, Pat," said McMoo with a reassuring smile. "We'll stay out of sight as much as we can."

The three cows left the Time Shed and sneaked into the palace through a nearby gatehouse. They shuffled along gloomy passageways lit by flickering torches. The chill of winter was in the stone, and they shivered as they clopped quietly up some steps towards the sound of chatter and laughter.

"Someone's having fun," Pat whispered.

Sneaking further along the corridor, they glimpsed several women folding sheets in a grand bedroom and gossiping.

"Chambermaids," whispered McMoo. "Let's listen in on their chat."

"What a boring waste of time," Bo complained.

Pat looked at McMoo. "Shouldn't we get on with finding the ter-moo-nator, Professor?"

"A chambermaid's job takes her all over the palace," McMoo reminded them. "They may well have *seen* the ter-moo-nator—"

"– and so they could give us a clue about where to find it." Pat gazed in awe at McMoo. "You're a genius, Professor!"

"True," agreed McMoo. With a wink, he led the two of them closer to the bedroom doorway.

"Just think," a lanky woman said as she plumped up a pillow. "The king's new wife is coming here this very night!"

"I hope she sticks around longer than the last one," said a spotty girl beside her.

"Of course," McMoo whispered.
"December 1539 – that means King
Henry is getting ready to marry his
fourth wife, Anne of Cleves. He ties the
knot on 6 January 1540 . . ."

"Oh, Molly, you *are* lucky being her
lady-in-waiting," the lanky woman
went on. "They say she's as lovely as a
summer's day . . ."

"Yeah, a summer's day when it's raining poo-poos!" The voice was gruff, sour – and very familiar. "Pah! Still, better get ready to meet her, I suppose. The king should be greeting her in the main hall any time now . . ."

Bo's jaw dropped. "That sounds like—"

"It can't be," squeaked Pat.

"It is!" McMoo murmured.

A large woman came thumping out of the room and wobbled off down the corridor with a sneer on her face. The cows ducked out of sight as she went past. She looked *exactly* like the dreaded Bessie Barmer!

"Clodhopping clover clumps," exclaimed Pat, trembling. "What is *she* doing here?"

"That girl called her Molly," Bo reminded him. "She must be, like, Bessie's great-great-great-great-great-great-grandmother or something."

"Bessie told us her ancestors mixed with royalty," McMoo remembered. "But she never said they cleaned the palace sheets and wiped the royal bottoms!" He turned round. "Come on – let's follow her to the main hall. I reckon the king will be the ter-moo-nators' target – we must do whatever we can to keep him safe!"

The cows trailed through the palace passageways, sticking to the shadows wherever they could. Eventually they found their way to a minstrel's gallery overlooking the main hall. Servants, lords and ladies were starting to gather there. Molly was one of them. She had a face like a dog's bottom.

"This is a perfect place to hide," said McMoo quietly. "From here we have a ringside seat for all the action!"

"No sign of the ter-moo-nators yet," Bo observed.

Then a young man in doublet and

stockings tooted a regal tune on a bugle. "All kneel for His Majesty!" he cried.

A set of wooden double doors swung open at the back of the hall, and McMoo snorted with excitement. "I can't believe we're about to see the most famous king in English history. Us – cows! Imagine that!"

A big, burly man in fine clothes strode into the hall. He had a huge head and a thick red beard, and he wore a flamboyant, fur-trimmed hat.

"There he is!" Pat gasped, peeping over the top of the gallery. "Wow, this is amazing!"

"That's Henry the Eighth?" Bo seemed less impressed. "He wasn't just fat, he was ugly too!"

"I wonder what Anne of Cleves will look like," said McMoo. "The history books say that Henry thought she looked like a horse . . ."

"And now, Your Majesty," announced the man with the bugle, "the woman you've been waiting for is here at last. She is, of course . . . Anne of Cleves!"

There was much applause as two figures entered the hall. To human eyes they looked perfectly normal. But because they were cows, the C.I.A. agents saw the newcomers as they really

were. One of them was wearing a garish green gown. The other was large and hunched and steel-grey, dressed in doublet and hose. Two spiky horns stuck out from his head. Both figures had pink snouts with rings through them.

"That's not Anne of Cleves," said McMoo grimly. "It's a clever heifer in a frock!"

Bo tutted. "Not even a *nice* frock. Look at that nasty embroidery!"

"Never mind that, look who's beside her," Pat spluttered. "It's the ter-moo-nator!"

Being unable to see through the F.B.I. ringblenders, King Henry noticed nothing unusual about his guests. Indeed, from the twinkle in his eyes as he gazed at "Anne", he clearly thought he was face to face with a total babe. "Well, well, well," he said, striding forward and taking her hand. "Aren't you a beauty!"

The cow gave a simpering giggle and allowed Henry to kiss her hoof.

"The F.B.I. are a cunning bunch," hissed McMoo. "They went back in time, intercepted the real Anne of Cleves and switched her for this impostor! *She* is the special F.B.I. agent Yak heard was being sent here . . ."

"But why?" hissed Pat.

"Isn't it obvious!" cried McMoo. "If King Henry marries a cow, it will become the queen of England. And Henry will find himself with the F.B.I. as his royal advisors!"

"England could become a power base for cows," Pat realized.

McMoo scowled. "And the history of the world would be changed for ever! Total chaos would result. The future as we know it would be destroyed."

"Oi!" Bo hissed. "Keep it down, Professor!"

But if anything, the professor was getting louder still. "How long before evil cows are sneaking into *other* royal families all over Europe?" he boomed. "The F.B.I. is mucking up the past – and if you muck up the past, you muck up the present and the future as well. They've got to be stopped!"

"Who goes there?" came an angry voice from down below. It belonged to the king himself! "Who's that yelling up in the gallery?"

"Now look what you've done!" Bo hissed.

The gathered crowd gasped in shock and fear as King Henry pointed a fat finger up at the gallery. "Guards, capture those intruders," he shouted. "No one may trespass here in my palace! If they try to resist – kill them!"

Chapter Eight

A DESPERATE PLAN

"Run!" yelled Professor McMoo.

Together with Pat and Bo, he dashed from the gallery and charged headlong down a dark, shadowy passage. On and on they ran. Then, as they passed a large window, the professor skidded to a stop.

Pat frowned. "What are you doing?"

"Come on, Professor," Bo complained. "While you catch your breath, the royal guards will catch *us*!"

McMoo ignored them both, forcing open the window with a snort of effort. Two storeys below was another courtyard. A large black horse was standing there, waiting to be stabled.

"Bo," said the professor urgently, "you must get out of here and find the *real* Anne of Cleves."

"But she could be anywhere!" Bo protested.

"So the sooner you start looking, the better!" He pointed down. "There's a stallion down there. If you get away on horseback you will cover the ground more quickly."

Bo looked down on the courtyard from the window and gulped. It seemed a long way down. "If I don't land on that horse, I really *will* cover the ground," she said, "in little pieces!" But already she could hear the crashing of guards coming their way. "Oh well. I suppose there's nothing else for it. Just look after yourselves, OK?"

"We will," said Pat, forcing a brave smile. "Good luck, sis."

Bo grabbed Pat in a clumsy hug,

placed a kiss on McMoo's snout – then jumped out through the window . . .

"*Geroni-mooooooooo!*" she cried as she plummeted to the ground. But luckily, her enormous gown billowed out like a parachute, slowing her fall. She landed right on top of the horse, which gave a startled neigh and jumped forward at full gallop. "Woo hoo!" Bo shouted, grabbing the reins and riding out of the palace grounds past startled soldiers.

"Your sister is quite a cow," murmured McMoo.

"She certainly is," Pat agreed proudly. "She'll find Anne, I know she will. But what are we going to do?"

"Simple," said McMoo. "When the guards come and find the window wide open and those soldiers milling about outside, they'll think that all us intruders escaped in the same way. Now all we need to do is find a place to hide, wait till the fuss has died down, then go and sort out that ter-moo-nator!"

"Is that all?" said Pat with a sigh.

"Come on, Pat." The thump and clatter of the angry guards was getting very loud now. "It's time to make like there's a matador coming to tea – and *run!*"

Together, the two C.I.A. agents charged off down the corridor.

An hour later, in the dark, deserted fields beyond Hampton Court, Little Bo slowed down her horse to give him a well-earned rest. She shivered with cold. How was she going to find the real Anne of Cleves? The silly woman could be anywhere.

Then, in the silvery moonlight, she spotted something on the ground close by. Something dark, round and sinister.

It was a large cowpat, still sticky and fresh.

"Of course!" Bo realized. "If I follow the trail of pats that the ter-moo-nator

and his girlfriend left behind, it should lead me to the place where they arrived.

Perhaps they're keeping Anne of Cleves there." She gulped as an awful thought struck her. "Or perhaps they've already killed her!"

The black horse looked at her oddly as if wondering why a cow in a gown was out in the cold, talking to itself in such a melodramatic fashion.

She sighed. "Good question." Swinging herself back into the saddle, ignoring the protesting neighs of her wobbly steed, Little Bo set off on the cow-turd trail. Was Anne of Cleves alive or was she pushing up daisies? Bo had to find out!

Chapter Nine

TRICKED, TRAPPED AND TER-MOO-NATED!

Pat jumped awake as a cockerel crowed. He had been dreaming he was back in his cosy shed on the farm. But now he had to face up to reality: he was trapped almost 500 years in the past, squashed up in a washing basket in King Henry VIII's laundry room.

"Makes a change from most Monday mornings," he mumbled.

Peering out from his basket, Pat saw Professor McMoo emerge from beneath a pile of crumpled bedsheets. They had been sneaking around the palace for most of the night, avoiding guards and trying to find ter-moo-nators. Then the professor had decided to come to the laundry room and hide till morning.

Pat yawned and stretched. "Shouldn't we start looking for the ter-moo-nator and his cow again, Professor? That fake Anne must be stopped before it's too late!"

But suddenly the door was smashed open – and they were the ones to be found!

"Well, well, well!" boomed a familiar voice. Pat gulped to see Molly the chambermaid standing there like a big lumpy barrel with bad hair. "Seems I have a pair of lordly loons in my washing!"

"Greetings, fair maiden," said McMoo quickly. "I am Sir Angus McMoo of Milkbelly, and this is . . . um—"

"Lord Pat of Luxembourg," said Pat quickly.

Molly frowned. "You look a bit like a cow, My Lord."

"As a child I was fed a lot of milk," Pat said truthfully.

"Well, whoever you are," said Molly, "it sounds to me like the two of you have got it in for Anne of Cleves."

Pat swapped a worried glance with McMoo. "She must have heard us through the door!" he hissed.

"Don't worry, Your Lordship, I don't like her neither." She wrinkled up her big, blobby nose. "Do you know how many times I had to empty her privy in the night? Ten times! Disgusting mess every time!" She frowned. "Strange thing is, it's more like a cow's business than a queen's, if you know what I mean."

McMoo jumped up, sending sheets flapping everywhere. "Molly, what would you say if I told you that Anne of Cleves is a cow," he said. "A cow in a cunning disguise? And that the king is in deadly danger?"

"Well really, My Lord!" Molly put a finger to her mouth. "I'd say – come with me and prove it! I don't want to waste my time looking after no cow. She's upstairs in her room now, still asleep."

Pat scrambled out of his basket. It was all he could do to contain an extra-loud moo. "Thanks, Molly! Lead the way!" He wished that Bessie Barmer could be so understanding and reasonable.

He and McMoo followed Molly impatiently as she wheezed and puffed her way along the dingy corridors. At last, they reached the right room.

"She's in there," Molly puffed. "See for yourself!"

McMoo sneaked quietly inside the posh guest bedroom, and Pat followed right behind. A large figure lay in the bed, dressed in a big white nightie.

"There she is, Pat," breathed McMoo.

Then he frowned. "But why would that miserable Molly be so helpful to a couple of unlikely lords she's never seen before?"

"Never mind barmy Barmer's ancestor," said Pat, pushing forward. "Let's take out this cow's ringblender and show the king who he's really planning to marry . . ."

But as he leaned over the figure, it turned to look at him. Its green eyes burned into his own.

"Pulsating potatoes!" he cried in surprise. "It's the TER-MOO-NATOR!"

The fierce-looking creature grabbed Pat's hooves in a crushing grip. "Got you," it hissed. "Puny C.I.A. fool!"

McMoo lowered his head, ready to charge. "Let Pat go!"

"Stay back, Professor," the ter-moo-nator warned him. "Or your young friend is history!"

Pat gulped. "I suppose that's a fitting

fate for a time traveller!"

McMoo glared at Molly in the doorway. "You tricked us!" he cried. "You allowed that ter-moo-nator to surprise us and gain the upper hoof!"

"Sorry," said Molly with a shrug. "But the foreign bloke with the funny eyes saw you sneak into the laundry room. He said he'd give me two sprouts and a bowl of beetroot if I got you up here. What a blag!" She held up her vegetable prizes with glee, then walked away. "So long, suckers!"

McMoo snorted and turned back to the ter-moo-nator. "Why bother to replace Anne of Cleves?" he demanded. "What are you planning?"

"Once our cow-queen has married Henry, the king will meet with a slight . . . accident." The giant grey bull smiled, its eyes blazing. "This will leave the cow free to marry a bull – and their calves will be heirs to the throne."

Pat gasped. "And so England will be ruled by cows forever more!"

"Correct," said the ter-moo-nator.

"But why lure us here?" asked McMoo. "Why didn't you tell the guards to get us in the laundry room?"

"You are clever. You might have talked your way out of trouble and convinced the king of the danger he is in." The ter-moo-nator gave a robotic snigger. "But when the king finds you here in Anne of Cleve's bedroom—"

"He'll be so angry he won't listen to a word we say," Pat groaned. "Professor, we're beaten!"

"Never say die, Pat," said McMoo. "And let's hope the king doesn't say it either!"

The next moment, guards poured into the room, pointing their swords at the intruders. And worse than that, King Henry himself was right behind them – as angry as an ogre!

"I dressed as Anne and took her place

to flush out your enemies, sire," said the ter-moo-nator quickly.

"So, that ugly old chambermaid was right!" roared the towering monarch. "Two intruders, here to do harm to my beloved Anne and her courtiers."

"But your beloved Anne is a cow!" Pat cried.

"How dare you?" the king thundered, his face turning redder than Molly's beetroot. "You shall DIE for this!"

"He said it." McMoo sighed. "Your Majesty, please. I must meet with you alone on an urgent matter—"

"Silence!" The king put his huge hands on his even huger hips. "The only person *you* will be meeting is the royal torturer – for an urgent *splatter*! And to avoid any further funny business, I shall marry my lovely Anne of Cleves in the Great Hall *this very afternoon*."

"But you can't, Your Majesty," cried McMoo. "You're not meant to get married until January!"

"A king waits for nothing!" Henry yelled. Then he looked at the ter-moo-nator. "You. Get out of that nightie, find Anne and arrange it."

"At once, Your Majesty," said the ter-moo-nator with a delighted smile. He let go of Pat, who stumbled helplessly over to the professor.

"Now, Guard Captain," the king bellowed. "Take these two nincompoops to the dungeons."

Pat gulped and McMoo glowered at the smiling ter-moo-nator as the guards grabbed hold of them and dragged them away . . .

Chapter Ten

THE TERRIBLE, TERRIBLE TORTURER

The dungeons were cold and smelly and slimy and dark. But Pat was quite glad there was no light. It meant he couldn't see the rats skittering about, or the mouldy skeletons of other long-forgotten prisoners.

"This is amazing," McMoo enthused. "Just think, Pat – a real Tudor dungeon!"

"I'm trying *not* to think about it," said Pat with a shudder.

"Don't worry," said McMoo soothingly. "They won't leave us here long."

Pat brightened. "Really?"

"Really." McMoo chuckled. "They'll take us to the torture chamber soon. A real Tudor torture chamber! Imagine that!"

'I don't *want* to imagine it," Pat cried. "How come you're so cheerful?"

"Because I have a crafty escape plan," McMoo explained. "I just hope they come sooner rather than later — and that Bo can find the real Anne of Cleves."

"Before it's too late," Pat agreed. "For us — and for the whole country!"

Finally, after what felt like for ever, a door opened with a noisy squeak and a chink of light spilled into the dungeon – along with half a dozen guards. They grabbed hold of Pat and McMoo and dragged them up a slippery stone staircase to a large, forbidding room.

The torture chamber.

Pat gulped. It was impossible to look anywhere without spying something horrible – a skeleton handcuffed to the wall, or a rusty thumb-screw, or an iron maiden lined with spikes. A large body-stretching rack stood beside a steaming cauldron of boiling oil in the middle of the room.

"What an amazing torture chamber!" enthused McMoo, grinning at his guards. "It's even nastier than I expected!"

"I'm glad you like it," came a scary, hissing voice from the shadows in one corner. "Because you may be staying here for some time . . ." The voice belonged to a stooped, ugly man, who now came shambling towards them. His face was a mass of festering boils, oozing warts and rotten teeth. "I am the master of your hideous fate!" the newcomer gurgled. "The designer of your despicable doom. Men call me

. . . the Terrible Nigel!"

"Nigel?" spluttered Pat. "What kind of name is that for a torturer?"

"A terrible one," McMoo remarked. "Which actually makes him the *Terrible*, Terrible Nigel."

"Hmm, I quite like that," mused the Terrible, Terrible Nigel. "Sorry to leave you waiting, my friends, but I was up half the night torturing a frog suspected of being a witch."

"Did it talk?" asked Pat.

"No," said the Terrible, Terrible Nigel. "I'm afraid it croaked."

"Can we just get on with the torture please?" said the guard captain impatiently. His men eagerly nodded.

"Fair enough." The torturer rolled up his filthy sleeves. "Now, then. Would you like me to start by pulling out your teeth or by pouring molten lead into a boot and sticking your foot in it?"

"Neither!" said McMoo firmly. "Never mind that frog you thought was a witch – *I* am a powerful warlock. And if you lay just one warty finger on me, I'll turn you into a farmyard animal!"

"Yeah, sure you will," scoffed the Terrible, Terrible Nigel.

"You expect us to believe that?" added the guard captain.

"I can see you need proof," said McMoo. He turned to Pat, winked and tapped him on the end of his snout.

Pat grinned. Suddenly he understood

116

what McMoo was up to.

The professor cleared his throat noisily and spoke in a spooky warble. "*Alacazam, alacazow, turn this fine nobleman INTO A COW!*"

At that moment, Pat snatched the ringblender from his nose. Without its twenty-sixth-century powers, everyone could see him as he really was: a bullock in fancy dress!

"EEK!" squeaked the Terrible, Terrible Nigel.

"Who else would like to be turned into a quite dashing bullock, then?" McMoo enquired.

"He really IS a warlock!" yelled the guard captain. "Get him, men! Now!" But his guards were too busy running about in a flap. One by one, they fainted with fright.

Seizing his chance, with a major-league moo, Pat butted the guard captain with all his might.

"YEEEEOWWWW!" The captain
landed bottom-first in the boiling oil
and shot straight out again! Hooting
and honking and holding his bum, he
tore around the torture chamber,
crashing into the few guards still
standing and knocking them down like
skittles. Finally he ran headfirst into the

iron maiden and conked himself out.

"That takes care of them," said McMoo. "But what happened to the Terrible Nigel?"

"The *Not* Terribly Terrible, Totally Rubbish Nigel you mean, Professor," said Pat, pointing with his horns. "He's hiding over there."

"Stay back," squawked the torturer. "I'm still in charge round here." He had curled into a ball and locked himself away in a very small cage. "Look, tell you what, we'll forget about pulling out your teeth and the molten-lead stuff for now, OK? How about I just whip you a bit?"

"Oh, do shut up, you nasty little nit!" said McMoo. Then he turned to Pat. "Quick – put your ringblender back in. Let's get to the Great Hall."

Pat nodded. "It can't be long now till the royal wedding."

"We must show Henry he's making a terrible mistake by marrying this terrible *Miss Steak*." Professor McMoo bounded up the stairs. "Come on. The future of the whole world depends on us!"

Chapter Eleven

THE STEAKS ARE HIGH

Professor McMoo flew through the palace corridors like a big beef missile, knocking aside anyone who got in his way. Pat followed close behind him. They *had* to stop the king's weird wedding – not just for the C.I.A., but for cows and humans alike throughout future history.

Luckily, McMoo had read about Hampton Court in his history books and knew the layout pretty well. Soon the two Cows in Action were nearing the splendid doors that led on to the Great Hall.

"Should we knock, Professor?" panted Pat.

But McMoo had already lowered his head and banged open the doors!

The grand, spacious room was cluttered with important guests dressed in their finest clothes. They scattered in noisy alarm as McMoo and Pat burst inside, making their way towards the

front of the hall – where King Henry was gazing happily into the eyes of a cow in a wedding dress, unaware of her "moo" nature. Molly and the ter-moo-nator hovered close by.

"Stop, Your Majesty!" yelled McMoo. "You are being tricked!"

"YOU AGAIN?" King Henry rose up to his full, formidable height. "Just who the devil *are* you, sir?"

"A friend to the king and an enemy to his enemies!" McMoo declared. He pointed his hoof at the ter-moo-nator. "And *that* crummy courtier is your true enemy!"

"Listen to the professor, Your Majesty," cried Pat, pushing forward to join McMoo.

"*Don't* listen, sire!" Molly urged him.

But King Henry was too furious to listen to anyone or anything. He turned to the nearest soldier. "Take these dogs away to the dungeons!"

Molly cackled like a witch, and the ter-moo-nator gave a grating laugh. "Well said, sire," he boomed.

"We are not dogs" cried McMoo defiantly as the king's guards charged towards him. "And that so-called woman in the wedding dress is *not* Anne of Cleves. She's a crafty cow in disguise!"

"There is no disguising your nincompoopiness, sir!" roared the king. "You shall rot in the Tower for such a gross insult!"

The guards seized Pat and McMoo.

"No!" said a shrill, female voice from the back of the hall. "Let them go, Your Majesty. Hear my words. The words of your *true* bride-to-be!"

The wedding guests gasped. Several of them fainted. Molly shouted some very rude words.

But Pat just mooed in delighted disbelief.

Because the voice belonged to a beautiful woman in a slightly crumpled dress, sat on top of a *very* exhausted black stallion. She was accompanied by three courtiers and a gum-chewing cow in a muddy frock – Little Bo!

King Henry peered through the crowd at these strange new arrivals. "And who might you be, madam?"

"She's the *real* Anne of Cleves, Your Fatness!" cried Bo.

"Little Bo!" Pat beamed as she trotted up to hug him. "You're all right!"

"Well done, Bo." The professor shrugged off his guards and joined in the group hug. "You found Anne – in the nick of time!"

As the black horse finally collapsed,

Anne jumped off nimbly. She led her courtiers through those few baffled guests who were still standing and squared up to the grim-faced ter-moo-nator. "This belligerent bull broke into my ship and left my courtiers and me tied up in a hut on Dover Beach," she said. "He took my wedding dress and gave it to this heartless heifer."

"Your Majesty," protested the ter-moo-nator. "Are you going to let these people insult your bride-to-be?"

"It's no insult – it's the truth," McMoo shouted. He marched up to the fake bride – and before anyone could stop him, he yanked the shiny nose ring from out of her snout.

There was a moo of alarm. Suddenly everyone in the hall could see the bride for what she was – a crafty cow!

A horrified gasp went up from those guests still conscious.

"What trickery is this?" spluttered King Henry.

"Don't let the King lock me up, McMoo!" wailed the cow.

"The F.B.I. made me do it! They twisted my hoof, honest they did! They said I would look good in a crown . . ."

But McMoo only shook his head sadly. He couldn't be seen to be talking to a cow. Now that her ringblender had been taken away, King Henry and his guests could not understand her words.

They heard only a loud, pitiful
"*Moooooo*".

Molly gasped, then groaned, then fell
flat on her back in a dead faint. Pat and
Bo cheered.

"You did it, Professor!" said Pat. "You
blew their cover and spoiled their plan!"

"Nonsense," said McMoo, pocketing
the F.B.I. ringblender. "*We* did it. All
three of us, together."

King Henry turned to the ter-moo-
nator. "What do you have to say for
yourself, sir?" he bellowed. "Before I
execute you?"

The ter-moo-nator simply scowled,
pulled something like a silver platter
from beneath his cloak and threw it on
the floor. "Mission abort!" he mooed
furiously. "One day, Professor McMoo,
you shall pay for this."

"Tell me when," McMoo jeered. "I'll
bring my credit card!"

"Recall!" rasped the ter-moo-nator.

"Recall!"

He and his not-so-special cow agent jumped onto the silver disc – which suddenly vanished in a puff of dark smoke. The few wedding guests who hadn't fainted finally managed to do so – along with the archbishop who'd been performing the wedding service.

McMoo sighed. "The ter-moo-nator and his cow have escaped back to the future."

"But at least we've kept F.B.I. agents off the throne," said Bo.

Pat nodded. "I wonder what the king will make of all this."

As it happened, Henry had hardly noticed a thing.

"Your beauty is blinding!" the king told Anne. "Truly, my dear, you are *not* a cow."

"Indeed I am not, sire," said Anne. She smiled as she turned to McMoo and Pat. "But please, Your Majesty, won't you pardon these loyal subjects? They are friends of the girl who freed me. I would never have reached you without her help."

"For you, my dear, anything." King Henry smiled at Little Bo. "Very well. The pathetic ninnies may go free."

"Cheers, King!" said Bo.

"Thank you, Your Majesty," said McMoo, and he and Pat bowed.

"You have my apologies," Henry went on. "And as I intend to marry this most marvellous un-mooish Anne of Cleves, you must all come to my wedding as my honoured guests."

"It would be our pleasure," said Professor McMoo. "But perhaps you should postpone this happy event until your guests recover." He checked a small history book he had stuffed in his pocket. "Um . . . How about 6 January at Greenwich Palace?"

"I'm not washing my hair that day!" Anne of Cleves smiled. "Sounds perfect."

"And so it shall be," said King Henry, taking Anne's hand. Her courtiers clapped politely, and Bo performed a wild victory dance.

"We did it!" Pat cried. "History is back on track!"

Bo nodded. "Cows in Action: one hundred million; Fed-up Bull Institute: nil!"

King Henry waddled up to them. "Now then, my new friends," he said gruffly. "Is there any way I can make up for my hasty actions earlier?"

"Well . . ." McMoo gave the king a big, broad bullish smile. "I don't know about anyone else, but I could murder a nice cup of tea!"

Henry looked puzzled. "Cup of what?"

"Oh dear, of course. How silly of me,"
said McMoo. "Tea won't be introduced
to England until 1658." Then he reached
into the C.I.A. sash under his outfit,
pulled out some tea bags and beamed.

"Luckily I brought my own supply!"

Pat grinned. "Professor, you are unbelievable!"

"But never un-*tea-leaf*-able!" McMoo replied.

Bo groaned. Anne of Cleves gave a puzzled smile. And King Henry grasped the tea bags in his big, clammy hands.

"Tea all round!" Henry boomed. "And let this happy day be celebrated till the end of time!"

Chapter Twelve

THE END OF THE BEGINNING

The king and Anne of Cleves enjoyed a quiet wedding in Greenwich followed by an enormous banquet. Little Bo had a quiet word with Anne and managed to get roast beef banned from the menu. And while the three unexpected guests from Luxembourg got some funny looks for eating so much grass, most of the lords and ladies were far too polite to say anything.

One person who was unable to attend was Molly the chambermaid. She was spotted by the Royal Chef guzzling her ill-gotten beetroot – unaware that the wicked bull had stolen it from the king's kitchens. Molly found herself blamed for the theft and, as punishment, she was sacked from her job as Royal Lady-in-Waiting – and told she had to clean all thirty toilets in the palace every day for a whole year.

"Serves her right!" Pat said.

And yet something was troubling Professor McMoo.

"Why the long face?" asked Little Bo, plonking herself down beside him and Pat. "*I'm* the one who should be grumpy. I've still got a swollen udder from all that riding I had to do."

"I'm just a little worried," McMoo replied. "In the history books, Henry thought Anne looked like a horse, remember? But she's really nice, and he seems delighted with her."

Pat suddenly understood his concern. "And the king is meant to dump her in six months' time, isn't he? Ready for wife number five."

McMoo nodded glumly. "So, what if we *haven't* saved history?" He looked over to where the king was sitting happily with a brimming flagon of wine and a chicken leg. There was an empty space beside him. "Where *is* Anne, anyway?"

"Relax," said Bo, a cheeky grin on her face. "She's on her way. I left her in her bedchamber."

"What were you doing there?" asked Pat.

"Since Molly's been sacked, I decided to stand in as Anne's lady-in-waiting." Bo shrugged. "Anne likes my style, so she asked me to give her a makeover for her honeymoon. She'll be down in a minute – wants to make a big entrance."

Pat clapped his hoof to his forehead. "A *makeover*?"

McMoo started to smile. "What have you done, Little Bo?"

Suddenly the doors to the banqueting hall swung open – to reveal a very strange sight. The room fell silent. The king choked on his chicken leg.

It was Anne of Cleves – wearing brown and white spotted flares and what appeared to be a long horse-skin

coat. She had a horse's tail pinned to
her hair, which was now dyed bright
purple.

"Hello, Henry," she said brightly. "What do you think of my new look?"

Pat grinned. "Not a lot, from the look on his face!"

"My love," croaked Henry. "You look like . . . like a *horse*! This is no way for the queen of England to dress."

"Oh, don't be such an old fuddy-duddy," said Anne crossly. "I think this outfit is fabulous. And it's all the rage in Luxembourg!" She grinned over at Little Bo. "Just wait till you see what I'm wearing tomorrow – a skunk-skin jacket with a slashed pink T-shirt, topped off with a hat made from ladybird wings."

The king buried his face in his hands.

"Don't worry, Henry," said Anne. "I'm going to have a matching outfit made for you!"

Henry's groan of dismay echoed around the banqueting hall.

"Huh!" said Anne. "Be like that then!"

And she stormed out in a huff.

"I can't see this marriage lasting long now," said Pat with glee.

"Nah," Bo agreed. "She's *way* too cool for him!"

"Nice work, Bo," murmured McMoo. "She will split up with the king, but lead a long and happy life as a princess of England with her own castle." He grinned. "And luckily, her funky fashion sense *doesn't* catch on!"

"I think it's time we left, Professor,"

said Pat as the king's advisors started muttering among themselves and staring at Bo. "We don't want to end up in the Tower of London for crimes against clothing!"

Together, the three cows slipped away from the hall to where a coach and horses were waiting to take them back to Hampton Court – and the Time Shed.

The moment they were inside, McMoo pulled the CHURN lever, transforming the empty shed back into an incredible time-craft in moments. And as the big computer screen swung down from the rafters, four familiar faces appeared there.

"Madame Milkbelly!" gasped Pat. "Yak! Shetland, Holstein!"

"What are you lot doing up there?" asked Bo.

"We are sending you a message from our own time," said Madame Milkbelly, looking down at them through her shades. "We want to congratulate you."

Holstein nodded happily, wearing his pointy hat at a jaunty angle. "Your mission was a success. The F.B.I.'s plan

has been defeated, and history is safe."

"For now," said Shetland ominously. His own hat was as straight as his face. "But the F.B.I. will keep trying."

Yak nodded. "There's gonna be other dangerous missions for you to face, troops."

"Bring 'em on!" said Bo. "We'll be ready for them."

"Too right!" added Pat.

"But for now, you must return to your farm in your own time," said Madame Milkbelly. "We will contact you again when we need you."

"Oh!" McMoo frowned. "But I wanted to escape the farm! I wanted to travel through time and never go back!"

Shetland shook his head. "The twenty-first century still has need of you, Professor. Your destiny awaits."

"See you soon," said Holstein, raising his hat.

Yak waved a hoof in farewell. "Ciao, cows."

"*Moooooooo*," added Madame Milkbelly.

Their pictures faded from the screen.

"Oh well," said McMoo with a sigh. "I suppose being the star secret agents in a secret organization of clever cows has its good points."

Bo nodded. "Getting to dress up in funky costumes, you mean?"

"And defending the future like no other animal on Earth?" Pat added.

"Well, yes, that too, of course," McMoo agreed. "But in particular I was thinking about an inexhaustible supply of those amazing future tea bags!" He kicked away some hay to reveal a neat stack of perforated sachets. "Twenty-

sixth-century tea is absolutely delicious. Stick the kettle on, Pat!"

Bo rolled her eyes. "Well, Yak was right about there being other dangerous missions to face. For a start — how are you going to land this thing back on the farm without Bessie Barmer noticing?"

"I'll simply land a split-second after we left," McMoo explained, throwing the switch that would take them home. "Barmer's even stupider than her toilet-cleaning ancestor – she won't notice a thing, just you wait."

The Time Shed rattled and hummed and buzzed and glowed – then shook as it landed with a thump.

"Here, little cows . . ." Bessie Barmer was calling, just outside.

"You did it, Professor!" cried Pat. "She still thinks the Prime Moo-vers are inside!"

"Quick, Bo," called McMoo. "The CHURN lever!"

Bo backed into the bronze lever with her bottom and the controls disappeared back into the walls, floor and rafters. The Time Shed became an ordinary shed again just in time – as Bessie Barmer barged inside with a big fork and a carving knife.

"Where are those stray cows?" she demanded.

"Mooooo?" said McMoo innocently.

"Moo," said Bo.

"Mooo-oo-ooo," Pat added, chewing on a bit of hay.

"And to think you're supposed to be the cleverest ones," grumbled Bessie. "Those strays must have slipped out somehow. Well, I'll find them and bring them to the butcher's – if it takes me all night!"

She stormed out and banged the door behind her.

"Ha!" said Bo.

Pat laughed too. "It will take her a lot longer than that to find Shetland and Holstein, eh, Professor?"

"Oh, yes – but I'm sure Yak and the Moo-vers will find us again very soon," said Professor McMoo, with a big, bullish grin. "Now we are fully-fledged C.I.A. agents, it'll be ACTION all the way – past, present and future!"

THE END

Collect them all!